A Twentieth Century Homunculus

By

David H. Keller

British Library Cataloguing-in-Publication Data
A catalogue record for this book is available from
the British Library

Contents

David H. Keller

David Henry Keller was born in Philadelphia in 1880. He studied neuroscience at the University of Pennsylvania's School of Medicine, graduating in 1903. He then served as a neuropsychiatrist in the U.S. Army Medical Corps during both World Wars, and was the Assistant Superintendent of the Louisiana State Mental Hospital at Pineville until 1928. In the same year, Keller travelled to New York City to meet with Hugo Gernsback, publisher of *Amazing Stories*, who bought his first professionally published science fiction story, 'The Revolt of the Pedestrians'. A year later, Keller was made Associate Science Editor of Gernsback's new magazine, *Science Wonder Stories*. This sparked Keller's most intensive writing period, which he combined with a small private psychiatric practice out of his home. Over the next two decades he produced eleven novels and more than fifty short stories, as well as a body of poetry and some non-fiction. Most of his work is regarded as far more complex and literary than that of his contemporaries, thereby foreshadowing the science fiction 'golden age' of the mid-20th century.

A TWENTIETH CENTURY HOMUNCULUS
by David H. Keller

As a result of being rather intoxicated, John Reiswick left the elevator at the twentieth instead of the thirtieth floor of the new Astor House. Immaculately dressed, drunk enough to be rather dignified, and at the same time, sober enough to keep quiet, he had started to attend a banquet, given in honour of the football team of Columbia University of the year 1937. This affair was being held just ten floors above the one in which the American Philosophical Society was holding its annual meeting.

Reiswick looked as much like a member of the American Philosophical Society as like an old football star of Columbia. Consequently, when he left the elevator at the twentieth floor instead of the one ten storeys above, obsequious waiters ushered him into the banquet hall, where he spent an hour of dreary eating in the company of two hundred real members of the Society. No one was certain of his identity, and so it was thought best not to take a chance of offending a distinguished guest, who was for the time being, apparently lost in deep thought. For this reason he had been placed in an advantageous position near the speaker's table. As much as his condition would permit, he gave serious attention to the programme, though the first few papers read made him wonder when the hip-hip-hurrah and the usual jollification would begin.

He really did not understand much of what was said and it was not till the last speaker was introduced that he heard anything of

4

interest. This member of the Society was a sociologist of note and the theme of his address was the gradual lowering of the birthrate in America. For some unknown reason the women of America were becoming sterile. Birth control, companionate marriage, feminine independence, the high cost of living, the diminution in the size of the average home, could be considered as playing some part in this lowered birthrate. It was believed, however, that none of these factors really reached the root of the trouble, and that unless the real reason was found for the rapid drop in the number of births and steps taken to correct it, the American people would soon fall from its commanding place as a leader of nations.

"There are not enough babies being born," the speaker said emphatically. "In fact," and here he tried to alleviate the seriousness of the situation by speaking in a lighter vein, "in fact, unless something is done soon, it may easily be that twenty years from now there will no longer be a football team at Columbia University."

John Reiswick has a one-track mind. That was what made him such a football star in the old days and the same trait had enabled him to become many times a millionaire in the ten years following his graduation. During these years, his great love had been the football team of Columbia and its supremacy over all other teams. He spent money as an alumnus as freely as he had spent his muscles prior to graduation. He worked at making money but he spent all his spare time increasing the glory of Columbia. Naturally, the part of the speech that seemed to impress him the most was that statement: "Twenty years from now there will no longer be a football team at Columbia University."

He remained quiet till the end of the programme, and then made a beeline for the sociologist. He simply asked for one thing—the man's card. In his alcoholic state, he could not do any logical thinking, but he did know that this man had made a statement that required investigation, and he also knew that the next morning he would have a clear head. With the card in his pocket, he left the banquet hall, as dignified and as drunk as when he entered it, but in that head of his was the one idea.

The morning came and with it sobriety. A shower bath and hot coffee put him in excellent shape for a day's work. His valet, who had, as usual, gone through his pockets, respectfully called his attention to a visiting card the rich man had brought home with him. At once Reiswick recalled the entire affair, and with the directness that had made him a rich man, he phoned to the office

that he would not be there till late, and started out on his search
for the speaker who had made such a disturbing statement.

Dr Stanfield was annoyed at being roused from a sound sleep
by a total stranger. He refused to see the man. This attitude did
not last long. The stranger was insistent—the stranger was worse
than that—he had stated bluntly that he was simply going to stay
there till he saw the Doctor and that no one was going to make him
leave. Realising, under the circumstances, that it would be better
to get rid of him by seeing him, Dr Stanfield sighed and wearily
dressed to go down stairs. Once down there, and finding who the
visitor was, he thawed considerably. He even told Reiswick that
he was glad to see him and asked him to breakfast. Reiswick
accepted the invitation and lost no time in giving the reason for the
early visit.

"What I want to know is simply this. You said last night that in
twenty years there would be no more football at Columbia. Why?"

The Professor frowned.

"That was rather a wild statement of mine. What I wanted to
do was to impress upon the Philosophical Society the danger of the
rapidly falling birthrate. There are thousands of women in the
United States today who are sterile, and, apparently, no scientist
has so far been able to discover the reason. Most of these women
want children and cannot have them. So serious is the situation that
the lawyers of the country have at least been talking about the
wisdom of passing a national divorce act which would allow an easy
separation in such cases of sterility. You see this lowered birthrate
threatens the very fabric of our national life. Our social security is
based on the continuance of the family. Our wealth has to descend
from father to son. The men of wealth feel that they have failed in
life if they have no son to inherit their estate. If the lowering of the
birthrate continues for another twenty-five years as it has for the
last five, the situation will become serious. In fact it is almost serious
now. If this is true, you can figure for yourself where the University
will get its football stars in another twenty years. As I understand
it many of the stars are from the families of the rich. It seems that
these are the families that are being largely affected. The very poor
seem to be having some children, but even they are not as prolific
as they were, and, of course, their children do not, as a rule, go to
our colleges and universities."

Reiswick shook his head rather mournfully as he murmured:

"No more football. Something must be done."

"No doubt something will be done. Someone will find the reason and with the discovery will come the cure. Are you a married man? No? Then you are in a serious condition. If you do marry, you are simply playing with fate. You will probable die without ever having a child you can call your own."

"You don't really mean that?"

"I really do. You have been so occupied with football and business that you do not realise the concern with which the New York upper set is looking at this matter. I have personally interviewed over one hundred physicians who take care of the best people in this city, and they tell me that a large part of their worry is the sterility of their patients. So far they have been unable to do anything. Their patients seem to be in perfect health, but there are no children."

"But there must be some way of solving this difficulty. We have to have men to keep up football at Columbia. And, now that I think of it, I ought to have a child. I am a rich man and I should have a family."

"I agree with you, but if you marry, the odds are against you. That was what I was talking about last night, and as far as I can see the matter is growing worse all the time."

"I shall have to think this over," said Reiswick, finally, as he drank the last of his coffee. "Send me a bill for this consultation and I will see that you get a cheque at once. I am going to see you again. This is very interesting to me, and I am going to see what can be done about it. It may sound conceited, but up to this time I have never failed to get a thing I started for. And I feel that I am going to get this."

As soon as Reiswick reached his private office he sent for his secretary.

"Bill, sit down. I want to talk to you. How many young men in the office?"

"Exactly one hundred and fifty-seven."

"How many are married?"

"As far as I know about fifty per cent."

"How many of them have had children this last year?"

"Just one."

"You don't mean just one?"

"That is all. And that is rather a peculiar case. Young Smithson in the shipping department. You remember that you sent him to

Burmah about two years ago? He married out there and, while he swears the little lady is a pure Aryan, she seems a little dark, though she certainly is pretty. I have seen her once or twice when she called at the office for her husband. They live over in Brooklyn and they have a baby three months old. You were busy coaching the team when the child was born and so, when the boys made up a present for them, I just put in fifty dollars for you and I never did think of telling you. It surely was of no importance."

"But it was. Send for Smithson. I want to go right out there and see that baby. No time to spend. Tell him I will be waiting for him in my auto out at the kerb."

"How about the letters, Sir?"

"You sign them for me. This is something far more important than the mail. I am up against the biggest problem in my life and there is no time to be lost. Do you know that I am thirty-three years old? I never realised the danger till now. You look after things while I am gone. Tell Smithson to hustle. I want to see that baby."

A few minutes later Reiswick and Smithson were in the automobile, threading their way to Brooklyn. The young shipping clerk was naturally excited. He wanted to ask a dozen questions, but realised that the best thing to do was to keep quiet till he found out what his employer wanted. Finally Reiswick asked:

"Why didn't you tell me that you had a baby?"

"I did not know that you would be interested."

"Not interested? Do you realise that I am more interested in babies now than I am in anything else in the world? I do not know when I was so interested in anything. How does it feel to be a father?"

"It really is wonderful," replied the young man, smiling. "You see, there are not so many babies in our neighbourhood, and it has brought us into a lot of social prominence. Lots of really fine people have called to see the baby and asked us to come and eat a meal with them and bring the baby. Several men have offered to buy the little one for as much as a hundred thousand, but of course we would not sell her for any amount. I think that she knows me already, and she is the most fun when she is taking her bath. I only have a chance to play with her at night and on Sundays. You see we are not rich enough to have a nurse and servants and so I help the wife a good deal. She does all her own cooking, knows how to make a lot of eastern dishes that are really very fine and not expensive either. Are you making this trip just to see a baby, sir?"

"Just to see the baby, Smithson, and that is all. I wanted to see a real baby and the first one I was able to locate was yours. As you say, babies are scarce. It has been a long time since I actually saw a baby. In fact, I do not remember when I saw a baby—real close. So I wanted to see one."

"Well, if you want to see a real baby, you will have a chance when you see Susanne. Takes after her mother some, but has my eyes and a funny little twisted smile. My wife says that she saw that smile when the baby was only a few days old, but then you know all mothers are foolish over their babies that way, thinking they look like the father. At least that is what I have read in the old books."

In another hour Mr and Mrs Smithson, John Reiswick and Susanne were entertaining each other in the bathroom. Susanne was having her morning bath—rather late—but then Mrs Smithson said that she always slept late. Reiswick just sat there and looked at the little girl. Finally, the rich man took a deep breath as he said:

"So, that is a baby?"

"I'll say it is," answered the proud father.

"She is my child," said the beautiful dark woman, in a very proud voice. "In my language I call her 'A Flower from God!'" She took the baby out of the water. Reiswick held out his arms.

"Please let me hold her for a minute."

And there the little one lay, looking up with wondering eyes at the big man playing with the golden football that hung from his watch chain. What passed between the baby and the old football star was hard to say, but no doubt it was a very important idea.

The rich man and the young shipping clerk rode back to the office in silence. As they left the automobile Reiswick said:

"I am going to double your salary. I want you to be able to take good care of your wife and baby. If she ever is sick, send for the best specialist and I will pay the bill. You are a fortunate man to have a child."

All that afternoon Reiswick sat thinking, in his private office. He refused to see anyone or to answer the telephone. At five he called up Dr Stanfield and asked him to take supper with him. The Doctor refused and pled a previous engagement. He was sharply told to break it, that there was a thousand dollar fee if he would give

Reiswick the evening. As a result, the two men dined in the millionaire's apartment.

"What I want is this," said Reiswick, "and I am not going to beat around the bush. I want to be a father."

"Why not get married?"

"You told me this morning that if I did the odds were against me. So why marry? I want at least an even break in any game I play."

"Well, you could try it."

"Too much gamble. I must be reasonably sure. There is no time to spare. I want a child just as soon as I can get one. I actually saw a baby this morning."

"Why not marry and adopt that child?"

"I am not rich enough. The parents would not sell it. They love it too much. It is interesting. The mother is from Burmah and does all her own cooking and housework. I actually held their little girl baby in my lap."

"Give me their address. I am investigating all interesting babies for the Rockefeller Foundation. We feel, if we can find out how some parents live and have children, that we may find the reason for other married men and women not having children."

"Go ahead. Here is his name and address. But such investigations take too long to please me. I want a baby at once and it would not be fair to a lady to marry her. I have to be sure."

"In other words you want to be a father."

"Yes."

"The important thing for you is not to have a wife but to have a child."

"That is it."

"You should have lived a few hundred years earlier. At that time ladies were not looked upon with much favour. Lots of scientists felt that the human race would be much finer in every way if there was only one gender, the masculine one. During that time there was a Doctor called Paracelsus. Some thought that he was a quack and then others were sure that he was a very wise man. If he were living today he might be able to help you, as he claimed, in one of his books, that he was able to make human beings without the help of the female sex. He called these interesting children by the interesting name of *homunculus*, and they were all men and all very brilliant mentally. I happened to think of it and brought the book with me."

"Stop your nonsense. The thing is impossible."

"It would seem so. Let me read you the exact description which he has left to us. Here are his directions to anyone who wants to follow them," and for fifteen minutes he read to Reiswick out of a very old, leather-bound book. Then he closed the book.

"He claimed that he made many of these little wise man and sold them to the nobility of Europe for Court advisers."

Reiswick scratched his head.

"I am not very well educated," he finally said. "I took the football course the four years I was at Columbia, but frankly, the thing seems impossible to me."

"It does to me, too," admitted Dr Stanfield, "but there is this to say about it. Here is an exact description of an experiment in biology. We look upon it as an impossibility but we have to admit that *no one has ever duplicated that experiment in this scientific age* and actually found out for themselves that it will not work. However there is a man out in Chicago who is doing some interesting things with frog's eggs. He takes the eggs and irritates them with a needle or with acid and every now and then one of them matures without being fertilised. This man is a recluse but he has done a great deal of work in parthenogenesis. I met him once and did not know whether he was insane or just queer. Perhaps you might induce him to do some work for you along the lines of Paracelsus."

"Give me his name and address," said Reiswick, rather grimly. "If money and science can give me a baby, I am going to be a father. You collect your fee from my private secretary. I am off to Chicago on the next train. If I go on the Pennsylvania I can fly from Cleveland to Chicago and save some time. I would like to talk more with you about this, but I am growing older every minute and have no time to spare."

In a most unceremonious manner he rushed out of the dining room and shouted orders to his valet. Before Dr Stanfield realised what had happened, he heard the front door of the apartment slam.

John Reiswick was on his way to Chicago.

Hermopheles Jones was working at a low powered microscope with frog eggs. One at a time he focused on them till he secured a perfect view and then with a very delicate needle he scratched the thin enclosing membrane. Now and then he broke an egg, others he scratched poorly. When he made a perfect mark, he smiled. He had decided to scratch fifteen hundred more eggs. If ten of them survived the injury and started to grow he would be satisfied; if two kept on growing he would be delighted.

Meantime his wife was working as a seamstress to support the family, including her husband and two aged parents. So far, there had been no children, and the learned biologist had been too much interested in frogs' eggs to appreciate this fact. He certainly did not worry over it.

He may have heard Reiswick speak to him, but he gave no sign of it. It is possible that he felt a strong hand on his shoulders, but he kept on working with the eggs. Suddenly, he felt himself lifted off the stool and forcibly dumped down in a chair. Standing in front of him a great man demanded if he was Hermopheles Jones.

The biologist glared at his visitor, as he replied:

"Yes, and you spoiled a perfectly good egg."

"Don't worry about that. I will buy you another one. I came all the way from New York to see you and I have no time to waste. I want to be a father. I want a baby."

"You let me go back to work. Are you insane? I don't have any babies. Go to an orphan asylum."

"Dr Stanfield of New York told me that you know more about eggs than any living man. Do you know about Paracelsus? Could you repeat his experiment and find out whether he was telling the truth or not?"

The scientist beamed his joy. Rushing over to the door he locked it and then returned to his visitor.

"Some think I am insane," he confided, "and if they knew what I really think they would be sure of it. Paracelsus? Do I know him? Why, man, that old scientist is my God. I think that he was one of the most wonderful biologists that ever lived. I have read and reread his work and the only thing that has kept me from repeating all of his experiments has been a serious lack of funds. Think how marvellous it would be! Life without the female sex! I have an idea that it would make *a perfect world!* Others can say that Paracelsus was a charlatan if they want to, but I really believe that he was able to do all that he claimed to be able to do. Now I have done a lot of work with eggs; I probably have done more with frogs' eggs than any living man, but I am too poor to work along the lines of that great Swiss."

"I have the money," said Reiswick, simply. "How much do you want?"

So then and there they talked the matter over.

Money can accomplish wonders. It is not surprising, therefore to find that Hermopheles Jones was torn from his Chicago retreat His family were amply provided for in every way for a three-year period. For the first time in his scientific life, the biologist was able to buy everything that he wanted to make a really accurate study of the primary source of life—from the masculine viewpoint.

A small island in an isolated part of the Pacific Ocean was bought at a fabulous price from the French Government. On this island a small, but wonderfully complete, town was built over night out of houses brought from San Francisco in sections. A colony of thirty persons, comprising every possible form of brains and labour required for such an undertaking, was transported from the States In all of these preparations, John Reiswick took a leading part as he was eminently fitted to organise and direct any undertaking In fact, he suggested several accessories to the equipment which had not entered the minds of any of the other members of the research group. One of these was a herd of goats with an experienced goat herder. Another was a small hospital, fully equipped for all emergencies and especially able to care for babies. Two graduate nurses were taken along to care for this hospital; also a young doctor to care for the health of the Colony and help entertain the nurses. Reiswick wisely said that since the final purpose of the expedition was to make him a father, it would be well to be fully prepared to care for the babies when they arrived. That was the real purpose of the hospital and of the herd of goats.

The rich man had so arranged his business that he could be absolutely free from any responsibility for at least three years. He wanted to have a real vacation. At the same time he was so accustomed to the conveniences of a modern office, that at the last moment he had added to the equipment an extra room fully furnished to serve as his office, even to the stenographer, who was to be his private secretary. As this idea had entered his mind but a few days before the ship sailed from San Francisco, he was unable to secure the services of a stenographer from his New York office and therefore was forced to employ one from the city of the Golden Gate. He realised that there would be little business to be transacted, but because he wanted to keep his mind occupied, he determined to follow out an ambition of years and write three books one a history of football, the other an account of the four years he had played at Columbia and the third a prophecy of what would happen to football in the future, if the continued disuse of muscles and the increased use of machinery made men smaller and weaker. He had devoted more time to sports in college than he had to literary composition, and therefore in his selection of a private secretary, he was careful to employ a young lady who was fully able in every way to assist him in the details of perfect literary work.

To say that Ruth Stilson was a modern girl in every way would have done her an injustice. She had not gone through the world with her eyes shut but she had kept her fingers carefully crossed, and devoted herself to the perfecting of herself in her life's ambition, rather than to the following of the bright pathways of the ultra-modern youth. All her life she had wanted to write a book; as a child, she was always scribbling on paper with a pencil; her study of stenography was a part of the preparation she made. In college, she majored in English, and her old professor openly stated that she had a better idea of the correct use of the comma than any student whom he had ever passed through his classes. She was not beautiful but she was brilliant from an intellectual standpoint; she was not modern but she never used the split infinitive; she did not live the life of a flapper, but she adored watching them. In fact she had composed a very serious essay entitled, "The Dynamite of Adolescence".

It was this very serious-minded young lady who was selected, from over fifty applicants for the position, to be John Reiswick's private secretary. After talking to her for a few minutes, the ambitious man felt that she was very safe socially, and at the same time would be remarkably helpful in the preparation of his manuscripts. She silently thrilled over the idea of three years on a tropical island, as she felt that the quiet and leisure would enable her to rewrite, and this time perfectly, her great American novel.

With his usual flair for organisation, Reiswick had overlooked no detail of the community life. The arrangements for feeding the colonists were complete, as two Chinese cooks served daily an abundance of every form of oriental fruit and vegetables with an occasional young kid, fresh fish or tropical fowl. Everyone had a definite work to do, and Reiswick had taken no one that could not do his work perfectly and at the same time harmonise with the other colonists. There was not only work but amusement for all. Early in the history of the island a series of sports were arranged and a request issued that each person spend at least two hours a day in exercise. A six-hole golf course was built, and Reiswick himself taught swimming to all who were not proficient in this sport. He felt that the only way for a healthy mental life to continue on the island was to keep everyone in the best possible physical condition. This was easy with all except Hermopheles Jones and the three wild-eyed biologists, whom he had induced to be his co-workers in this great life-adventure. These four scientists would never have left the workshop had it not been for the insistent demands of the great American who was spending several million in this biologic effort to become a father in the shortest possible time.

Reiswick had several serious conferences with Jones. The biologist, as is the case with many ultra-scientists, did not seem to comprehend the real urge behind the spending of these millions of dollars. He showed this in one of his remarks to Reiswick.

"I consider the hospital inadequate," he exploded. "In fact, the whole economic machinery is too small. We should have conducted this experiment in a great city where there would be adequate facilities for the care of hundreds and thousands of babies at the same time. If this experiment works at all, we are just as likely to have fifty thousand babies growing to maturity as we are to have one. What should we do with them? What good would thirty goats do? By the time we imported a ship-load of milk, those perfect children of my skill would die of hunger. Besides our laboratories are not large enough, our glassware is inadequate. You should have listened to me."

"You do not understand my purpose," replied Reiswick, calmly. "I want to be a father, but I have no special yearning to be the father of fifty thousand babies. In fact, I feel that *if I had just one* I would be satisfied, especially if it was a boy baby. That was one reason why I was interested in the statement of Paracelsus. All of the babies he made were males. Of course, if we made fifteen at the same time and sent them all to Columbia at once and formed a Columbia-Reiswick football team, it would be a rather fine performance, but I am not as enthusiastic about football as I was, so I am not going to be disappointed if the baby you make for me *is a girl*, so long as she grows to be as beautiful a woman as my mother was. Of course, back of everything, is a desire to do something towards preventing the human race from going out of existence, but primarily I regard this as purely formative experimental work of a very personal nature. If you can make one baby, there is no reason why you cannot teach the scientists of the world

how to make babies in every large city, and in that way the race
will be preserved. Of course we may only be able to make males,
but perhaps they can get wives—in Burmah. So you keep this in
mind. I want to be a father, but I do not want you to overdo it.
I'll stop the whole work and discharge you if you start turning out
these babies like a—like a—well, like a swarm of bees."

The scientist threw up his hands in hopeless dismay as he said:

"But what am I to do? Suppose we are successful and we have a
thousand babies in the first experiment? Do you want me to kill
them—these beautiful results of my scientific skill?"

"My mother used to warn me never to cross a bridge before I
came to it. So far you have not made even one baby. In fact you
tell me that you have not even started to make a baby. You wait
till you actually have a thousand babies and then you come to me
and we will decide what to do. We may pick out ten or twelve of
the finest ones and concentrate on them."

"Then you are not going to let me grow fifty thousand if I
can?"

"Certainly not! Think how it would make me feel to be the
father of fifty thousand boys and some of them girls! There are
not enough names for that many. We would have to give them
numbers and tattoo them to tell them apart. Miss Stilson would
have to devote all her time to making a card index for them. Why,
I should have to endow several universities just to educate my
children, and then—think of this. I am not the richest man in the
States. There are others with far more wealth than I have, and
when one of us starts a new fad, they all enter into the most active
competition. Suppose it became known that I was the father of
fifty thousand children? At once three or four other men would
never be satisfied till they had a hundred thousand apiece and the
large banking houses like Morgan's might try to have five or ten
million. It just would never do. There might be an actual over-
production. That is why I selected a desert island for this work and
pledged everyone to secrecy. That is why I look over all out-going
mail. So do not be too rash in your enthusiasm. I shall be satisfied
if I have just one baby to call me 'Papa' and I am going to love it
just as much if it is a girl as though it were a boy."

When Reiswick returned to the office he repeated as much of
this conversation as he could remember to his secretary. One of
his reasons for having an office and a private secretary was to
enable him to keep an accurate diary of the work of the colony.

For this reason he made Jones dictate a daily statement of his progress. Of course the work was so ultra-scientific and the language used so pedantic, that no one could have any idea of what it meant, except an equally learned biologist, but Reiswick wanted a record of the work to stand as a text-book for other men in their efforts to keep the human race from final dissolution.

More and more Miss Stilson became interested in the efforts that the big man was making to become a father. She became so enthusiastic that she spent long hours going over every detail of his ambition. She even cried a little as he told her of the years which had passed without his even seeing a baby, and then of the great thrill and deep longing that had come over him when he held the little child of the Burmese woman in his arms.

"I knew then," he told her in the direct language that he was always in the habit of using, "that wealth makes no difference and fame is at best a temporary gesture. Ambition can be selfish. I found when I touched that little baby, that after all, love is one of the great emotions in life. Since my mother died I have had no one to love me or to love—and it seemed to me that if I had a child, it would make life worth while. That is why I am spending three millions of my money and these three years of my life here. Many of the colonists think that Jones is trying to make gold or a medicine to prolong life, but what he is really doing is more valuable than gold and makes life really worth the living. I should rather be a poor man, like my shipping clerk, and have the love of a child, than be worth all of my millions."

"As I remember it," remarked the secretary, "your shipping clerk was married and this child of his was a natural child, the result of the great love that can exist betweeen a man and a woman."

"Yes, she was a Burmese woman, but very beautiful. They were poor, but devoted to each other. It is peculiar how attached people can be when they are in love with each other even when they are poor. They had no servants and she did all the cooking in the oriental style. He said that he would rather listen to his wife talk and his baby coo than live in a fine hotel without them."

"Then they were in love?"

"That is what they said. I offered to buy the baby but—nothing doing! Right then and there I made up my mind to have a baby of my own. I wanted to be a father."

"Do you really believe that if Hermopheles Jones is successful and makes a baby for you, after the method described by Paracelsus, you will be satisfied?"

"I believe so. I guess so. Of course it would be nicer to have a baby—well, like my shipping clerk did—but the best authorities say it is a great gamble nowadays. To use their own language, 'An increasing number of women are showing idiopathic sterility'. If I married, there would be no surety of being a father and I could not be cruel enough to divorce my wife just because she happened to be unfortunate."

"But you would appreciate a wife. The more I think of it, the more impossible your position seems. Take the affair from the viewpoint of the child. That baby is entitled to a mother just as much as to a father. What are you going to tell the poor little thing when it grows up? Now if you had a wife, she could mother the little baby, even if it was of this peculiar Paracelsian origin. Then when the baby grew up it would have *parents* instead of just a father. It would be like other children and that would make it happier. Then there is the attitude of society. You disappear from your friends for three years and when you come back you have a little baby. How are you going to explain it? Are you going to tell your friends that it is a Paracelsus baby? They will think that you are insane. But if you have a wife you can simply say, 'This is our baby' and your friends will say, 'What a lovely child. She resembles the father but she has her mother's eyes.' Do you see? There would be no need of any awkward explanations."

"I never thought of all that," answered Reiswick. "I am a one-track man. All I can think of now is to become a father. After I really have a baby, I suppose these other matters will come to my attention and then I will deal with them as the necessity arises."

For some months he worked very hard on his three books on football. As a result he saw a good deal more of Ruth Stilson than he did of any of the rest of the colonists; in fact he saw more of her than he had seen of any woman during his entire life—except his mother. His secretary's intelligence made him envy her; her interest in his desires to become a father pleased him and her ability to turn his dictation into beautiful English made him determine that under no circumstances would he ever permit her to work for any other man. In other words, he fell in love with her and did not realise it. That is, he did not know it till one day she was in swimming and was stung by an electric ray fish. She suffered so she became unconscious and Reiswick had to bring her ashore, where the Doctor worked for some time to resuscitate her. During those anxious moments John Reiswick understood what it would be to be deprived of her companionship for a lifetime instead of a few minutes of unconsciousness. He now realised what was the matter with him.

The following Sunday they were married by the Episcopalian clergyman who had been brought along to look after the spiritual needs of the little colony. Without doubt this marriage was one of the most noted events occurring on the island. The cook served a wonderful dinner, the ladies of the colony did their best to furnish adequate floral decorations and combined all their wardrobes to make the bride's wedding dress. Even the four biologists were forced to take a full day's vacation.

After that came three glorious months of tropical sunshine and lovely nights, illumined by the moon and stars and melodied by the ceaseless throbbing of the surf on the complaining coral strand. The longer John Reiswick and his bride lived together, the fonder they became of the poetry of life, and the less interested they became in football and the great American novel. At times Reiswick even lost sight of just why they had come to the island.

Then came the regular semi-annual visit of the private steamer. The Captain brought confidential messages that made the happy bridegroom go around with a long face. There was danger of war being declared between the United States and Japan. Of all the rich men of America, Reiswick was the only one that wielded a powerful influence with the little brown men of the Orient. The President urged him to go to Japan and stay there till a better understanding could be arrived at between the two great powers. It was a request that could not be ignored and Reiswick at once saw that the only thing he could decently do was to comply with the request. He dreaded to tell her, but he felt that it would not be wise for her to go with him. War might be declared at any time and there was the danger of submarines. To his surprise she was willing to remain on the island; it seemed that she was afraid of being seasick, and besides, she felt that it was her duty to stay on the island and look after his interests while he was away. She considered that there was too great an investment there for both of them to go and leave it. She ended her argument by saying:

"Hermopheles Jones seems to feel that he is actually making some progress. He is always saying, 'Time will tell', and is remarkably optimistic. If he really does produce a Paracelsian baby in the next year, all the more reason for one of us being here to direct its care. So you go, and come back as soon as you can, and take good care of yourself, because I love you—and I am just going to die if anything happens to you."

That was the end of the argument. Reiswick gave a multitude of orders, a large amount of supplies was unloaded, and then the steamer slowly disappeared into the western seas. Ruth Stilson Reiswick cried. She had not known that love could hurt a woman so much.

Six months and some weeks passed. Reiswick was a go-getter. He had gone to Japan to stop the war-talk and promote a kindlier feeling between the two nations, and he had finally succeeded. The Japanese Emperor had decorated him with the Order of the Rising Sun. The medal was a beautiful gold star, encrusted with diamonds, and when Reiswick first looked at it, he suddenly realised what a wonderful plaything it would make for a baby. The word, baby, recalled the island and the biological Jones and the lonely bride, Ruth, who was so patiently waiting for his return, and, in the meantime, looking so efficiently after his interests. He radioed the President of the United States that all was right in Japan and that he was leaving to look after his personal interests. Then he boarded his steamer and told the Captain to put all the steam on and beat it for the island.

He arrived at the lonely island just at twilight. The Captain urged him to stay aboard ship till the next morning, but he refused and ordered a boat to take him ashore. Arriving there, he walked rapidly to his home. There was no one there; there was no one in the office. Then he saw lights in the hospital building, and went there. A group of colonists were seated on the steps. The Preacher took Reiswick to one side and told him in grave tones that Mrs Reiswick was sick, but that everything was being done for her that was possible. The excited, worried man rushed into the hospital, but was told that he could not see her; not now, she was too sick. He asked a hundred questions to which no one seemed to be able or willing to give him any satisfactory or definite reply. At last he walked back to his office and sat down in his favourite chair; the chair opposite him was the one his wife used to sit in when they were working on his books. He wondered how life would be if she never took any more dictation? What had he done to deserve this? Why had fate made it necessary for her to die just when he had come back to her?

Then Hermopheles Jones came in. He seemed as downcast as Reiswick. At the same time, he said that the experiments were going along all right and that they were at a point where he might be able to announce success at any time. He said that at times he was discouraged; it seemed rather hard to follow Paracelsus in some of his experiments, the language was ambiguous, but at the same time they were making progress. Reiswick heard him as though a spirit were talking across the table. Finally Jones said:

"Have a drink? Will you take one if I fix it?"

"No. I am through with that sort of thing. Ruth does not like it."

Then he remembered that he should have said, "Mrs Reiswick".

They sat there through the night. Finally the morning came, as it does come in the tropics, with a great burst of light, like a flower of the dawn, suddenly unfolding from the bud. Reiswick heard the sound of laughter, confused voices, and wondered if the women were hysterical. Great God! That was it. Ruth was dead and they were coming to tell him and it was too much for them. They were laughing and crying. She had died and he was not there with her at the last moment. It was cruel of them to shut him out. A nurse came running into the room and in her arms was something in a blanket, and the white-gowned woman said:

"Oh! Mr Reiswick and Mr Jones. It's a girl and the finest you ever saw. What do you think of that, Mr Jones? A baby on the island."

The rich man was torn between emotions. His wife was dead and, in spite of the pessimism of Jones the biologist had produced a baby. Through his tears, he smiled at the little man and wrung his hand.

"I congratulate you," he said. "This will make your name immortal. It was your brains and perseverance that enabled you to show the world that Paracelsus was right."

He turned to the nurse.

"Take good care of this baby. See that it is neglected in no way. Start the goat's milk according to the Doctor's orders. As soon as advisable I am going to have her baptised, and I am going to call her Ruth after my poor wife. You can all understand how I feel about this; the success of the experiment leaves me cold; if it had happened before the illness of my wife, I should have been the happiest man on earth. Now please leave me. I want to spend a few minutes with my dead wife, the only woman who has loved me since my mother died."

They gathered around him and tried to tell him something. He simply shook his head, like a stricken lion, and burst through them in his wild rush to the hospital. The nurse slowly followed him, carrying the baby. Up the steps and into the room that had the odour of chloroform. The Doctor blocked the door and the Doctor landed outside the hospital on the ground. Then, into the room, Reiswick went and fell on his knees by the bed.

Eternity passed, and then he felt a hand straying through his hair.

"No one should do that but Ruth!" he said and turned to reprimand the nurse, but he found that the hand was Ruth's hand as was the wan smile. She was not dead at all. Not at all! She had just been sick but she was better now. Wonderful. Fine! Exquisite! Ruth was alive and Jones had a baby for them, a little girl baby, AND HE HAD ALWAYS WANTED A GIRL BABY.

"I am glad you came back," whispered the wife.

"I came just in time."

"It was the baby pulling you back."

"It was God bringing me home to you."

"Are you glad, Johnnie, about the baby?"

"I certainly am. Jones is to be congratulated. It is all working out nicely. You are going to get well and the baby will have a mother."

"It's our baby."

"You bet. That is what we are going to tell her when she grows up. No use in her knowing about this Paracelsus stuff. How about it though? Shall I tell Jones to go ahead and make fifteen or twenty more?"

"Right now I think that one is enough," whispered Ruth Stilson Reiswick. Her request was a command to the rich man.

He looked up at the nurse who was holding the baby.

"You let me have that baby and you go and tell Dr Jones I want to see him."

In no time the biologist entered the room. Reiswick faced him, and in the millionaire's arms the baby slept.

"Dr Jones. You have done fine, and from what I have seen of this little baby, whom I am going to legally adopt as my daughter, she comes very nearly being a real fine child in every way. I congratulate you and I will see that you are kept in comfort for the rest of your life. If you want to, you can go ahead with your studies. It may be that you can arrange with the French Government to supply them with a hundred thousand babies, but, as far as I am concerned I am ready to stop. My wife and I have talked this matter over and she thinks that even fifteen babies would be too many. So I want you to dismantle the workshop. Everything in it belongs to you. We are going to close this colony and as soon as Mrs Reiswick has recovered from this strange illness, we will go back to New York."

"You want me to stop?"

"Yes, as far as I am concerned."

"Right when I felt I was on the point of success?"

"Yes. I consider that you and I have shown that Paracelsus was right. If the work is to be conducted on a large scale, it will be in some other place than this island."

The biologist left the room. Reiswick sat down beside the bed and held his wife's hand. On the other side of the bed the nurse sat holding the baby. Mrs Reiswick looked at her husband.

"So you really are glad?" she said.

"I certainly am. I consider it a triumph for Dr Jones and that grand old man Paracelsus, and of course I deserve some praise as I supplied the money and the inspiration."

"Don't you think I deserve some credit?" asked the wife.

"Why Ruth! What do you mean?"

"Silly!" she cried.

In the course of time the colonists landed in San Francisco and the three Reiswicks started at once for New York. As soon as they arrived there John Reiswick went to see Dr Stanfield. That man gave him no time to say a word.

"I am certainly glad to see you. I want to tell you the news, but no one seemed to know where you were or at least were not willing to tell if they knew. Right after you left, we investigated the case of that shipping clerk and his baby and we were impressed with the fact they were eating an entirely different variety of food than the average American family was eating. We had suspected that this wave of sterility might be caused by a vitamin deficiency and so we worked their diet out from this viewpoint. We isolated an abundance of a vitamin which we will call No. 6 and we found that we could produce it very cheaply. We experimented on several thousand cases and the results were fine. The information was spread by the Government and we see now that there is no need to worry. So it would have been all right for you to have gone ahead and marry. Did you go somewhere with Hermopheles Jones ? The last I heard was a rumour that you and he were going to duplicate the experiments of Paracelsus. Did you do it ? Did you produce a baby ?"

"You bet we did," replied John Reiswick, with a grin.

www.ingramcontent.com/pod-product-compliance
Lightning Source LLC
Chambersburg PA
CBHW030535020726
47494CB00004B/1371